The Adventures of
Energy Annie

Book 1

Elizabeth Cosmos

Illustrations K. Henriott-Jauw

Ama Deus Energy Press
Lowell, MI

For Tyler, because he asked.

Ama Deus Energy Press
P.O. Box 93
Lowell, MI 49331
ama-deus-international.com

ISBN: 978-0-9962780-4-1 Printed book - hard cover
ISBN: 978-0-9962780-5-8 Printed book - soft cover

Illustrations by K.Henriott-Jauw
Editing by Christopher Cosmos
Design and layout by Anita Jones, Another Jones Graphics

Publisher's Cataloging-In-Publication Data
(Prepared by The Donohue Group, Inc.)

Cosmos, Elizabeth.
   The adventures of Energy Annie. Book 1 / Elizabeth Cosmos ; illustrations, K. Henriott-Jauw.

   pages : color illustrations ; cm

   Summary: "Together with her family, friends and pets, Annie explores and shares her eventful days
playing and learning. Then one day she discovers something new which draws her into the invisible
world of energy and changes how she sees herself and the world around her."
   Interest age level: 005-010.
   ISBN: 978-0-9962780-4-1

   1. Healing Energy--Juvenile fiction. 2. Vital force--Juvenile fiction. 3. Spiritual healing--Juvenile fiction.
4. Healing Energy--Fiction. 5. Vital force--Fiction. 6. Spiritual healing--Fiction. I. Henriott-Jauw, K. II. Title.

PZ7.1.C676 Ad 2016
[E]

"Bye, Mom! Bye, Timmy! I am going to the park with Mitzie!"

"Annie is coming!" Sally yelled.

"OH NO! "Annie! Are you alright?"

"I do not know... ahh Mitzie are you here?
I cannot breathe and my vision is blurry."

"Annie, what happened, did you trip?" asked Sally. "I do not know, all of a sudden my chest felt funny and I could not breathe." Tommy spoke up, "That's really weird, I think you should tell your parents!"

4

"You are shaking Annie. Come on, we will walk you home."

After the doctor listened to her lungs and heart with a stethoscope,
she asked, "Annie, can you describe what happened yesterday on
the playground?"
Annie recalls her strange episode to the doctor with her family.

"W-e-l-l, I was running with Mitzie to the park. Then I felt my chest get heavy and I tried to breathe, then my eyes went blurry. Then I was on the ground with Mitzie licking my face. I could hear my friends shouting my name."

"Well, from my examination, and your story Annie, it seems that you had an asthma attack. I would like to send you home with an inhaler."

"An attack?" asked Annie.

"Yes Annie, this is how we describe a sudden episode of not being able to breathe. The next time you feel this start to happen, use this inhaler."

"And what is asthma?"

"Asthma is when the muscles around your breathing tube tighten and makes it difficult to breathe."

"My parents do energy healing, and it really helped when I fell off my bike last week."

"And, yes, I am sure the energy healing would help you to relax, but the inhaler is for a real emergency if you cannot breathe. And you should keep this close to you."

"You mean I have to take this to school?"

"Yes, it would be good for your teacher to have the inhaler during school in case this happens again."

"Asthma Annie is here."

"You are quiet this evening, Annie.
Was everything ok at school today?"

"School was just fine, but someone teased me about the inhaler. I heard someone whisper Asth-ma Annie. That did not make me feel good. I was thinking maybe the energy healing would help me. I see you use this for your headaches, Dad, and Mom I see you use this on Timmy. I would like to learn how to use my hands for healing like you do."

"We can arrange for you to work with our instructor, we were only waiting until you asked."

"But you do not talk about how this is done. Most of the time I see you just close your eyes. I thought it was secret."

"It is not a secret, Annie. But the way is kept sacred. This is why you do not see the steps we take."

"What do you mean sacred?"

"That is a good question, Annie. All of life is sacred. We have a Divine Creator, and all of life comes from this invisible, all-knowing Source. This Source or spiritual energy is all around us in the air we breathe, the leaves and trees, the birds in the sky and the worms in the ground. We simply need to learn how to be in tune with this ever-present energy to stay in balance."

"Even Mitzie?" Annie asked.

"Everything, even the rocks, the plants, the water, the stars, moon and sun."

"All are made by one Divine Creator. Anyone can work with energy from the Divine Creator, and everyone respects and takes special care when working in this way."

"When can I learn?" Annie asked.
"Maybe this Saturday while we work in the garden. We will ask Ms. Katie to see if she is available to instruct you, just like she did for us."

"Will I still have to go to the doctor?"

"Oh, the doctor has a place for the care she prescribed, and we are very grateful," Dad answered. "There is a place for medical doctors, chiropractors, acupuncturists, and herbalists. But right now, you seem eager to learn more about yourself. There is a place for self-care, too. Self-care begins with the understanding that we are more than our physical body. There are very fine, intelligent bodies of energy or light that are also part of you."

"Oh, I know what you are talking about. I see shimmering light around Mitzie, and especially my little brother. Is this the invisible world you are talking about?"

"Yes, Annie, some people can see these energies, and others just feel them. When you begin to look at everything from this bigger energy world, you begin to really see how everything is connected. Everyone has the ability to understand and sense their entire energy field. Along with your physical body, a beautiful body of light expands out farther than your extended arms. Many times you will hear this called your subtle light field. Doing things like yoga, qigong or meditating helps to keep your entire self balanced. The doctor can help you feel better, but you have the ability to stay balanced and heal. Do you understand the difference?"

Mind

Moods

Body

Shimmering
Energy Layers

"Yes, healing is about all the parts of me working together: my mind, my moods, my body A-N-D the other shimmering energy layers. Medicine helps in critical emergencies. Right?
See I A-M ready."

Finally, Saturday comes. Annie is very excited to listen to Ms. Katie and learn about energy healing.

"Annie, have you scraped your knee before?" "Oh yes, many times, especially when I am climbing trees."

And what's the first thing you do?"

"Hmm. Well, I first put my hands over the spot and hold tight and close my eyes."

"Yes, that's what most people do. This is such a natural reaction, to put our hands on places that hurt. It is also natural to place our hands on people when we care and give hugs. I am sure you have done this with your baby brother, right?"

"Oh, yes. And when Timmy gets his bath, he always gets a mini-massage. I like rubbing warm oil into his skin. He makes the sweetest sounds and gives us a big smile."

"Yes, our hands are extensions of our hearts, Annie. You felt a special feeling when your mother placed her hands around you when you were so frightened telling the story of not breathing at the park. This feeling is Love, and is most easy to feel in your heart. Your heart is the place that constantly fills with Grace and Joy and Happiness from our Creator"

"Is this how my mother and father work with this love energy?"

"Yes, Annie, and so do I, and so will you. I will share with you a prayer, or what we call a spiritual routine, that will connect you to this feeling in your heart."

"My father says that energy is everywhere and in all things."

"Yes, this is true, and sometimes this is difficult to understand. We do know that for thousands of years, all over the world, different peoples in places like Egypt, China, our Native Americans, Tibet, and the Amazon, have been doing sacred healing. Your parents and I learned a way of healing from native people of the Amazon. Do you know where the Amazon is?"

"YES! There is a very large jungle and river in South America called the Amazon. Will we have to go there?"

"Oh no, we will begin by lighting this candle and creating a similar ceremony right here, just like it has been done for thousands of years."

"Ceremonies help our minds and hearts to work together. In this ceremony you will receive a transmission of energy. This transmission gives a clear connection to the Divine Creator. Then we learn a special prayer that turns the healing energy on for us to use any time we ask. Sort of like when you need water, you turn the faucet on and water comes through the garden hose."

"So the prayer connects me to the energy?" asked Annie.

"Yes, Annie, exactly how this works is a great mystery, for sure, but we can try to make examples. A garden hose is one example. The water from your hose comes from an underground spring. When we wish to water the garden, we turn the faucet on, which opens a pathway for the water to flow. Another example is this electric socket on the outside of your house. Your mother has told you not to touch this as it has a very strong current of energy. You may safely plug a power tool in, or a light, and presto, you have electric energy. You cannot see it, but the energy is always there, to use at any time. You just flip on the switch. Same with using Divine energy, we cannot see it but the presence is always there for us. So once you are connected with this all-knowing divine Source, you then flip the switch on by saying a specific prayer. Your hands are the power tool."

"I am ready!" said Annie.

"Then let us begin this short ceremony and learn the prayer. Then you can practice on me."

"Now that you have learned the steps, remember this is sacred and is done in reverence and silently to yourself. Just like you see your parents doing. Please, Annie, would you practice on my sore shoulders!"

"Sure!" said Annie. Then she begins to focus and hears a whisper in her ear, "Annie, you are a child of the Universe, you are being showered with loving golden grace to give you strength to help change this state."

"Oh, Annie, this came very easy for you! Take care of this gift.
And thank you, my shoulders feel so much better!"

"I could feel something, Ms. Katie! And I heard someone talk to me."

"The feeling, Annie, is the flow of loving energy that is doing the healing. What you heard is your guardian angel, or what some people call their spiritual guide. Everyone has one. And they help when you ask. Because of your prayer and caring heart, your guide is here to assist as the healing energy flows to the needed area."

"Mom, Dad! I love this! It is so easy. Here, Mom, sit down,
let me show you what I have learned."

"Oh, Annie, I would love something calming, thank you!" Annie closes her eyes to begin her spiritual routine and feels the energy building. She hears the whisper once again, "Annie, you are a child of the Universe. You are being showered with loving golden grace to give you strength to help change this state."

"Mitzie, I am s-o-o-o thankful I am not Asthma Annie any more. I
am so much bigger than I imagined. I am Energy Annie!
This is so wonderful!"

Activities

Parents, please look at these following ideas and explore together!

1. Look at the first pages of Annie's energy field and see how this changes with what she is thinking or doing throughout the book, especially as she is learning to work with energy.

2. Can you describe the personal guide for Annie and her teacher Ms. Katie, or her brother and others?

3. Have you found the word "energy" on each page?

4. Parents take the opportunity to have conversation around our Mind Body Emotion and Spirit bodies (on pg. 15).

5. With your own paper trace the outline of this physical body and subtle energy field and color your own page of how you sense your subtle energy field to be. Maybe create some changes.

6. Now draw how you sense or see your personal guide, your guardian angel.

7. Turn the page and explore Annie's neighborhood.

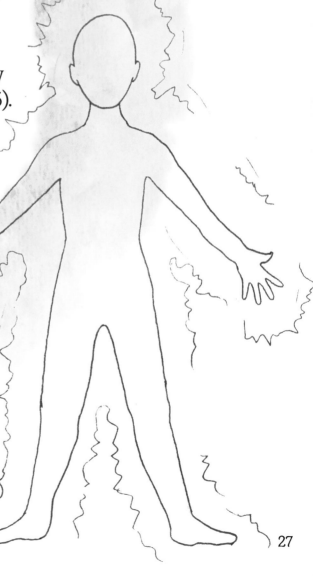

This is Annie's neighborhood. Do you see all the different stores and public buildings in town? Annie lives in a green house with her parents who meditate. Her father likes to do QiGong before work, and her mother goes to the yoga studio while Timmy naps. Annie's family goes to the neighborhood garden plot where they tend organic vegetables.

Very often other families are there at the same time. One neighbor has chickens and sells eggs. Annie's grandparents keep bees and have fruit trees, and Annie helps to sell honey and fruit with them. Annie walks to school. She plays at the park near the giant maple tree and sometimes she and Mitzie walk to their special field. Can you find these places?

Watch for me in Book 2, coming soon

The Adventures of
Energy Annie
Learning Respect

CPSIA information can be obtained
at www.ICGtesting.com
Printed in the USA
BVHW020230141118
533104BV00009B/18/P